To my three favourite
little lions,
Amy, Ellie and Lizzie

E.C.

First published 2015 by Macmillan Children's Books,
an imprint of Pan Macmillan, a division of Macmillan Publishers Limited.
20 New Wharf Road, London N1 9RR.
Associated companies throughout the world.
www.panmacmillan.com
ISBN: 978-1-4472-5742-4 (HB)
ISBN: 978-1-4472-5743-1 (PB)
Text and illustrations © Emma Carlisle 2015
Moral rights asserted. All rights reserved.
A CIP catalogue record for this book is
available from the British Library.
2 4 6 8 9 7 5 3 1
Printed in China

Lion Practice

Emma Carlisle

Macmillan
Children's
Books

My name is Laura and I love to practise.

I love kangaroo practice,

boing boing boing!

parrot practice,

flap flap flap!

and elephant practice too.

whoooosh!

And I'm VERY good at crocodile practice.
Everyone thinks so.

Mum says that today
I should practise being
something small and
quiet, like a mouse.

But I have a
much better idea.
Today I will try...

Lion practice!

Lions walk on their
hands and feet, like this...

And lions have the messiest manes, like this...

PERFECT!
But what else?

I think lions are good at hiding,

and leaping,

and running VERY fast!

oh, and I know,
lions roar REALLY
loudly, like this...

OAAAR!

But mum and dad didn't
like my roaring,
or my leaping.
They told me to
stop running
around and
keep the
noise down.

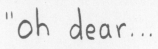

I'm sorry...

I just...

"... I just wanted to
be a good lion."

Dad came out
and found me...

...and then mum came too.

"Don't be sad, Laura," they said.

"Guess what we've
been practising?"

BIG BEAR HUGS!
For our favourite little lion."

A little lion?

A little LION!

What else do little lions do?

Mum says they need
a BIG dinner.

And dad says they need extra
bubbles at bath time.

I say little lions
don't like pyjamas.

Mum and dad
say I can be a cheeky
monkey sometimes...

A cheeky monkey?
That sounds like fun!

I'm going to practise being
one of those tomorrow.